E
COH

Cohen, Miriam

See you in second
grade

$11.95   10126

DATE			

© THE BAKER & TAYLOR CO.

See You in Second Grade!

STORY BY MIRIAM COHEN

PICTURES BY LILLIAN HOBAN

 Greenwillow Books, New York

Watercolor paints were used
for the full-color art.
The text type is Souvenir.

Library of Congress Cataloging-in-Publication Data

Cohen, Miriam.
See you in second grade!
Summary: At an end-of-the-year beach picnic, Anna
Maria, Jim, and the other children realize they
will miss First Grade and their teacher, but
decide they are ready for Second Grade after all.
{1. Schools—Fiction.   2. Picnics—Fiction}
I. Hoban, Lillian, ill. II. Title.
PZ7.C6628Sd   1989   {E}   87-14869
ISBN 0-688-07138-4
ISBN 0-688-07139-2 (lib. bdg.)

FOR JENNA BRUNTVEDT, FIRST GRADER,

WHO GAVE ME THE IDEA

"Old MacDonald had a farm, eee-yi--eee-yi--o!"
The bus driver and the teacher's aides
were singing, too.
First Grade was going on their
end-of-the-year picnic to the beach.

"I go way down in the ocean," Danny told Jim and Paul.
"I just do like this."
  And he started swimming on the bus.

"Once, when I was little, I went to the beach.
When I saw the ocean I started to cry
because it was so big," Sara told Margaret.

"I can smell it! I can smell the ocean!" cried George.
"It smells like French fries!"

The teacher said, "I think that's the refreshment stand at the beach, George. But that means we're there."
"Yayyyy!" the whole bus yelled.

Anna Maria jumped out first.
"I'll show you the bathhouse
where we change," she said.

But then she looked in her shopping
bag and saw—her big brother's
sneakers and jogging suit!
She had taken the wrong bag!
Anna Maria started to cry.

No one in First Grade had ever
seen Anna Maria cry, except when
she was telling on somebody.

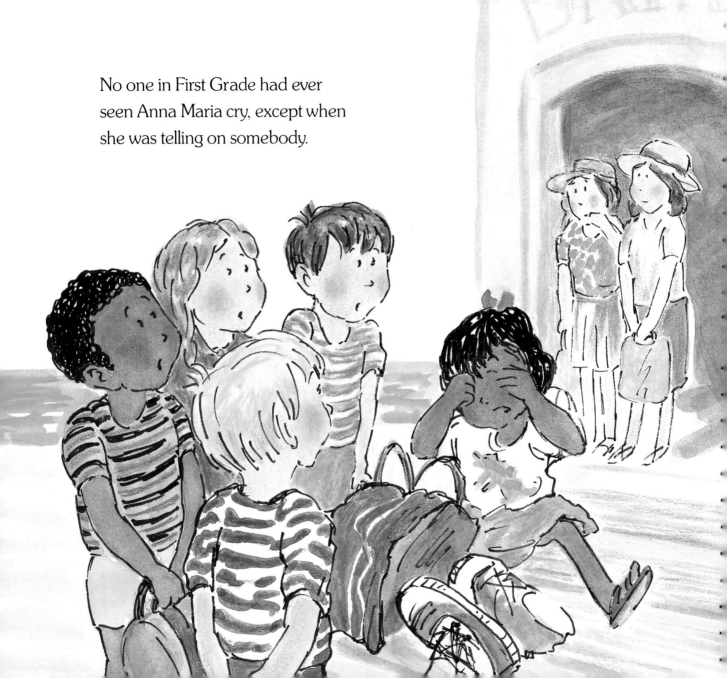

Sara said, "You could wear your dinosaur tee-shirt in the water."
"But what about the bottom?" Anna Maria said.
  She cried some more.

The teacher said, "You can wear your panties.
I don't think anybody will know the difference."
Anna Maria shook her head and went on crying.

"Oh, what a pain!" said Danny.
"Here. You can wear my shorts
after I put on my bathing suit."
Anna Maria stopped crying.

When they had changed, everybody rushed to the ocean.
Danny ran right in. He slapped the water
and jumped up and down, yelling.

Jim and Paul lay on their stomachs with their legs
straight out and their hands walking on the bottom.

Sara stood on the shore watching Margaret.
"Come in the water! It's fun!" Margaret called to her.
Sara didn't want to say it, but she was afraid.

Then Anna Maria came out of the water.
"I'll take you," she said.
She took Sara's hand, and they lay down by the edge
of the water and let the little waves wash over them.

Their teacher called, "Lunch time!"
They all ran up the beach and sat down on the sand next to her.
"Anna Maria's lunch was in her bag," said the teacher.
"But if we share our food there will be enough for everybody."

So they all got to taste each other's lunches—
Willy's cream-filled cupcakes, Margaret's
jelly doughnut, Jim's tuna sandwich, and
the teacher's cream cheese on rye bread.

After lunch they sat watching the ocean and talking.
"Do you remember," their teacher asked, "when we
went to the museum and some of you got lost?"
"Yes!" they all cried.

"And when we had a costume party, and Jim
pushed that Zoogy into the wastebasket?"
Willy and Sammy said.
Everybody remembered something.

Then Willy said, "Maybe it's going to be
too hard in Second Grade."
And Margaret and Sara sat closer to the
teacher and leaned on her.
"I wish we could stay in First Grade
with you forever!" said Sara.

Their teacher shook her head. "It's good to go into Second Grade because you are ready to learn new things. But I will miss you," she said. "You know, I've had fifteen First Grades and I've never forgotten a single one of my First Graders!"

Their teacher smiled at all of them.
"Now let's pick up our picnic papers and
put them in the trash," she said.

Then they changed back into their clothes,
except Danny. He said he didn't mind
wearing his bathing suit on the bus.

"This old man, he played one.
  He played knick-knack on my thumb," they sang.
  And "There's a little white duck swimmin' in the water!"

But after a while they didn't sing any more.
Everybody was sitting next to a friend
and thinking. Jim felt a different feeling
than he had ever felt before. It was serious,
being old enough for Second Grade.

When the bus stopped their
parents were waiting.

Danny jumped off and shouted,
"See you in Second Grade!"
He ran off without looking back.

Jim got up. "We'll all come back and see you when we are in Second Grade," he told their teacher. Then he and the others got off the bus and waved and waved before they went home.